# Troubles in the Rain Forest

**Elaine Pageler**

**High Noon Books**

ORDER DIRECTLY FROM
ANN ARBOR PUBLISHERS LTD.
P.O. BOX 1, BELFORD
NORTHUMBERLAND NE70 7JX
TEL. 01668 214460 FAX 01668 214484
www.annarbor.co.uk

# Contents

Nate and Nell's mother is an ecology professor. During the year, Dr. Kidd teaches at a college. When summer comes, people invite her to meetings all around the country. Nate and Nell often travel with her.

"Ecology is man and nature living together in harmony," their mother always says.

Nate and Nell smile. "And we're the Kidds who help," they say.

# CHAPTER 1

## The Amazon Rain Forest

The telegram came during lunch at the Kidd's home. It read:

> *Dear Dr. Kidd:*
>
> *Your friend Torbi and his family are in trouble. Can you come down?*
>
> > *Captain José*
> >
> > *Manaus, Brazil*

Dr. Kidd called her college and asked for a week's leave. Then she phoned her sisters and her aunt. None of them were home.

Dr. Kidd turned back to Nate and Nell. "No babysitters," she said.

"Why can't we go along, Mom?" Nate asked.

"We're studying about South America in school. The trip would help us," Nell added.

"Yes, it would. I have to be back in a week so you wouldn't miss much school. O.K., let's pack. The 'Ecology Kidds' are going to the Amazon rain forest," their mother told them.

"Hurray!" shouted Nate and Nell.

The next morning they were flying over South America. Nate and Nell watched out the window. For hours the ground had looked like a green mat. Now the plane started lower. They could see the ground better.

"Trees! Trees! Trees! That's all there is," Nell said.

"What do you expect? It's the rain forest. There's a river. Is it the Amazon, Mom?" Nate asked.

His mother shook her head. "That river is much too small. There are many rivers because it rains a lot. They all flow into the Amazon," he said.

Nate knew his mother liked to talk about South America. "This is the biggest rain forest in the world. Isn't it, Mom?" Nate asked.

"That's right, 54 percent of the world's rain forest is here. The Amazon rain forest covers two-fifths of South America," Mom answered.

Nate thought of the world map at school. "That's big," he said.

"It sounds big. But rain forests are getting smaller all the time. People cut them down. In 1950, 15 percent of the earth was covered with rain forests. Now, only half is left," she said.

"That's a big change," Nell said.

Mom nodded. "It worries me a lot. This rain forest has the largest collection of plants and animals in the world. And one-fifth of all birds live here. There are plants and animals we don't know about yet. Many of these plants might be used to cure sick people," she told them.

"What happens to those plants and animals when the forest is cut down?" Nell asked.

"There's nowhere for them to go. Another problem is that burning rain forests causes some of the earth's warming. Also, the forest blots up the rain. Floods happen when the trees are cut down," Dr. Kidd said.

"Then why do they cut them?" Nell asked.

"Some people don't think of the value of the rain forest. They just want to make money. A lot of furniture is made from rain forest trees. Others are used for fuel. They also clear the land for farming and grazing cattle," Mom said.

Just then, the loudspeaker came on. "Fasten your safety belts. We will land in Manaus, Brazil, in ten minutes," the voice said.

Nate glanced out the window and saw a big

river. There was also a large city cutting into the forest. It had high-rise buildings.

"I thought Manaus would be a small jungle town," he said.

His mother shook her head. "Manaus is a big port. Ocean-going ships come up the Amazon," she said.

Nell frowned at all the tall buildings. "Does Torbi live here?" she asked.

"Yeah, I hoped to go into the rain forest," Nate said.

His mother laughed. "Don't worry. We won't see Torbi until tomorrow. By then we'll be deep in the rain forest."

# CHAPTER 2

## Learning About Torbi

The Kidds spent that night in a hotel. The next morning they took a taxi to the waterfront. Big ships were docked there. Men and machines rushed to load some and unload others.

"These docks look different," Nate said.

"Yes, they're built on floats because of so much rain. They go up and down with the level of the water in the river," Dr. Kidd told him.

The taxi driver made his way through the workers. He drove along the waterfront.

Mom pointed to one of the small boats tied here. "There's Captain José," she said.

The Kidds got out of the taxi. The weather was hot and muggy. Nate felt damp all over.

A man wearing a captain's hat hurried off the boat. "Hello, Dr. Kidd. I've been watching for you," he called.

He shook hands with Dr. Kidd. Then he turned to Nate and Nell. "I don't believe it. Are these your twins?" he asked.

Mom nodded. "Captain José, this is Nate and Nell. I thought they would find this trip interesting. So I brought them along. My husband died three years ago. Since then, my children have traveled with me a lot."

"Going with Mom is fun," Nate said.

"We see exciting places," Nell added.

Captain José smiled. "Yes, I bet you do. But there's nothing more exciting than the rain forest. Let's get your things on board. We pull anchor in a few minutes," he said.

The boat was old and looked like a raft loaded with boxes. There was one bench for passengers. A small roof covered it and the captain's wheel.

"Captain José takes people and supplies up and down the river. His boat is the only one that docks at Port Sagra," Dr. Kidd said.

Captain José grinned. "I gave your mother her first trip into the rain forest," he said.

9

Mom nodded. "That was before your father and I were married. I was doing field study here," she said.

"Did you meet Torbi then?" Nate asked.

"Yes, he and his family are forest people. I came across their village one day. They knew the rain forest and were a great help. I stayed with them and finished my study," Mom said.

"Your mother helped Torbi and his family buy their land," Captain José added.

"That was later. I came back for a short study five years ago. Your father was alive then," Mom said.

"I remember," Nate said.

"So do I," Nell added.

"People were talking about clearing the forest for farms. Torbi was afraid his family might have to move. I got a loan for him. It helped him buy a small part of the forest. He and his family pick and sell Brazil nuts. That way they can pay off the loan," Mom told them.

"I love Brazil nuts!" Nate exclaimed.

"Then you're going to the right place. Torbi should have them harvested now. They may be on the dock when we get there," Captain José said.

"What's the trouble with Torbi?" Mom asked.

"Actually, there's not much to tell. I was docked at Port Sagra three days ago. Torbi paddled up in his dugout canoe. He said he was being forced to sell his land," Captain José said.

Dr. Kidd was shocked at this news. "Did Torbi say why?" she asked.

"No, Carl Klumt and his cousin Harve walked up just then. Torbi quickly said to tell you. He paddled away fast," Captain José said.

"I've never met Carl and Harve Klumt. Who are they?" Mom asked.

"They're farmers. Their land was cleared after you were last here. It borders Torbi's forest," Captain José told him.

Dr. Kidd looked worried. "Let's get started. I need to stop Torbi from selling his land," she said.

Captain José pulled up the anchor. "We're on our way," he told her.

*Captain Jose pulled up the anchor.*
*"We're on our way."*

13

# CHAPTER 3

## Going up the River

Captain José steered the boat upstream. The sky had clouded over, and the rain fell straight down. Nate and Nell watched from under the roof.

"You'll see a lot of this. It's the rainy season now," Captain José told them.

"Is that why the river's muddy?" Nate asked.

"Yes, it's also why Brazil nuts are being sent down river now. The nuts were ready earlier but people like Torbi need lots of rain to get down their small streams," Captain José said.

Nate saw baskets on the decks of many boats coming down. They must be filled with nuts.

"The Amazon is a busy place," Nate said.

"Actually, this is the Rio Negro. Rio means river. It joins the Amazon ten miles below Manaus. Yes, it is very busy. Rivers are the highways here," Captain José told them.

Up ahead there was a fork in the river. Captain José turned onto a much smaller stream. Now the trees crowded the banks. They were like huge walls on either side. Below them, Nate saw an alligator sunning on the bank.

After a few miles, they came to a village.

Captain José pulled up to the dock. A woman and a girl waited there.

"That's Carl Klumt's wife and daughter Jan. They must be going home to Port Sagra," Captain José said.

He unloaded some boxes on the deck. Then the woman and girl came aboard. Soon the boat was moving upstream again.

Nell and Jan smiled at each other. They became friends right away.

Captain José made stops at more villages. He unloaded boxes at each place.

"Port Sagra is the next stop," he said.

Mrs. Klumt looked at Mom. "Our village is very small. It only has a store and a few houses.

16

Where are you staying?" she asked.

"With Torbi's family," Mom told her.

Mrs. Klumt looked surprised. "Torbi and his family live in grass huts in the forest. You could stay with us. There's a hiking trail to his village. It's only a few miles," she said.

Mom shook her head. "I've stayed there before. We have brought hammocks with us."

"At least let Nell stay with us. Jan would love to have her," Mrs. Klumt said.

"Oh, yes," Jan exclaimed.

"Please, Mom?" Nell asked.

"Jan needs company. Also you can see those rain forest farms," Captain José whispered.

"O.K., Nell can stay tonight. We will walk

over and get her tomorrow," Dr. Kidd said.

"Come for lunch," Mrs. Klumt said.

"Port Sagra is ahead," Captain José called.

Nate looked in surprise. The clearing was smaller than the other villages. It only had a dock and a few buildings with tin roofs. The biggest one must be the store.

Two men waited at the dock. One stood near a muddy jeep. The other had a cart.

"Hi, Luis. I have supplies for your store," Captain José called.

Mrs. Klumt pointed to the man near the jeep. "That's my husband. Would you and Nate like a ride to the trail?" she asked.

Mom shook her head. "Nate and I will

paddle up the stream." She turned to Luis. "May we borrow one of your dugout canoes?" she asked.

"Sure, it's very good to see you again, Dr. Kidd," the storekeeper answered.

Mom and Nate went to the jeep and met Carl Klumt. The farmer had a kind face.

"Don't worry about your daughter. We'll take good care of her," he said.

Meanwhile Captain José helped Luis unload. "Have you seen Torbi? His Brazil nuts should be waiting on this dock," he said.

"I haven't seen him," Luis said.

Captain José turned to Dr. Kidd. "I don't like this," he said.

"Neither do I," Dr. Kidd answered.

## CHAPTER 4

## Torbi's Home

The dugout had been carved from a tree. Mom and Nate pushed it in the water. They climbed in and paddled off. Soon this stream forked, too. Two dugouts were pulled up on the bank.

"That's new," Dr. Kidd said.

She paddled past and turned onto a narrow stream. Trees and vines hung over the water so close that Nate could reach out and touch them.

Thousands of hidden birds were singing. There was the sound of chattering, and limbs cracked high above. It must be monkeys.

Nate stared into the dark forest but all he could see were more trees. They must be 100 to 150 feet tall. Most had no lower limbs. Their upper branches blocked out the sun. Huge vines hung down from them.

"That's called the forest's canopy (CAN-oh-pea). Many plants and animals live up there. We don't know much about them," Mom said.

Now Mom pointed to the thick ferns and shrubs living on the forest floor. "They're called the understory. They need very little light."

Nate and his mother paddled on. Butterflies darted past. Insects swarmed around. Nate brushed them away and wiped the sweat from his forehead.

There was an opening in the trees ahead. Three dugouts were pulled up on the bank. Some forest people stood there watching.

"Dr. Kidd!" they shouted.

Three men hurried out of one of the grass huts. The older one rushed over to Mom. "Thanks for coming, Dr. Kidd," he said.

Mom shook his hand. Then she turned to Nate. "Torbi, this is my son," she said.

Torbi shook hands with Nate and led him to the two men. "These are my sons and their wives and children," he said.

Nate smiled at the forest people. They grinned back at him.

*"Torbi, this is my son,"* Mom said.

Now Dr. Kidd turned to Torbi. "What's the problem, my friend?"

" My harvest of Brazil nuts was stolen. That's why I must sell. Without nuts, there is no money to pay the back the loan."

"Stolen! How did this happen?" Mom asked.

"Last week we loaded our boats with nuts. Then drums sounded in the forest. We all went to see who it was. First the drums came from one way. Then they came from another. We spent all morning looking and didn't find anyone. The nuts were gone when we got back."

"Who would do that?" Dr. Kidd asked.

"I don't know. Carl Klumt and his cousin Harve asked to buy my land. Now I'll have to sell," Torbi said.

"No one has sent nuts on Captain José's boat. They must still be at Port Sangra. Where did the drums come from?" Dr. Kidd asked.

Torbi led them into the forest. He cut thick bushes with a machete (mah-SHET-ee).

Mom pointed to a tall tree. "Look, Nate, there's a Brazil nut tree," she said.

Nate looked around him. All the trees seemed to be different. "Don't Brazil nut trees grow in groves?" he asked.

"Trees don't grow that way here in the rain forest. One square mile may have 3,000 kinds of trees," his mother said.

"The drum noises came from this way.

When we got here, they came from another direction," Torbi told Dr. Kidd.

Nate saw something shiny peeking through the ferns. "What's that?" he asked.

Mom pushed the ferns away. There sat a tape player. It had a tape of drums inside. Also, it had a timer.

"Here's your drums. The timer was set to play only for a short time," Dr. Kidd said.

Torbi inspected the tape player. "No forest person knows how to do this. That only leaves Luis or the Klumts," he said.

Mom nodded. "Don't worry, Torbi. We'll find those nuts," she told him.

**CHAPTER 5**

## Farms in the Rain Forest

That night Nate and Mom hung up their hammocks in one of the grass huts. Outside, the forest was alive with sounds. Screeches, screams, and howls echoed in the trees.

"It's animals. They hunt at night," Dr. Kidd said.

Nate was sure he would stay awake all night. But soon he fell asleep.

The next morning Nate and his mother headed for the Klumt's home. Torbi went along and led the way through the forest.

Finally they came to a muddy road. Up ahead the land had been cleared. The soil looked red and sandy. Most of the crops had been washed out by the rain. The plants that were left didn't look healthy.

Carl Klumt walked toward them. "I suppose you've seen my fields. There's not much of a crop this year. The first year was fairly good. But every year got worse."

"Rain forest land isn't good for farming. The soil is not rich," Dr. Kidd told him.

"You are right. Farming here isn't good. Also, my wife and daughter get lonely. But let's not talk about my problems. Lunch is waiting,"

Carl said.

He led them to the house and they went inside. Nell ran toward them. "Jan and I had a wonderful time," she said.

Another man waited nearby. He looked like Carl but his face wasn't so friendly.

"This is my cousin, Harve. His farm is down the road," Carl told them.

Harve shook hands with Mom. "Nell says you have been to the Amazon before," he said.

"Yes, part of my study was on this land. It was a beautiful forest," Mom told him.

"We enjoy farming here. A friend wants to join us. That's why we've asked Torbi to sell his land," Harve said.

Dr. Kidd was surprised at this. "Have you told your friend about the trouble growing crops, Carl?" she asked.

Carl looked away. "Our friend isn't worried about that," he said.

Harve turned to Torbi. "How about it, Torbi? Would you like to sell?" he asked.

"Torbi told you no. Why would he change his mind?" Dr. Kidd wanted to know.

"You can never tell. People change their minds sometimes. Just let me know if you do, Torbi. The offer still stands," Harve said.

Mrs. Klumt came out of the kitchen with a platter of food in her hands. "Let's eat," she said.

Lunch was very good. Afterward the Kidds

and Torbi started home.

Mom stopped and stared at the fields again. "I can't believe the Klumts would let a friend come here to farm. They'll all starve," she said.

"It's not a friend. I heard them talking. They want to sell out to a cattle company. But the Klumts need one more farm for the deal," Nell told them.

Mom frowned. "Cattle companies are buying lots of cheap land in the Amazon. It doesn't matter if the land is poor. They raise cattle and sell beef to fast food places," she said.

"And I'll have to sell to them," Torbi sighed.

"Maybe not," Dr. Kidd told him.

31

## CHAPTER 6

## More Answers

Torbi took a detour on the way back. He plunged into the dark forest. "Come. I have something special to show you," he said.

Dr. Kidd, Nate, and Nell followed. Ahead was a rare shaft of sunlight. There was a hole in the canopy of trees. Torbi pointed to the forest floor. There lay a big tree.

Nell gasped. "Oh, see those beautiful flowers! They look like orchids," she said.

"Yes, they sure do," Nate agreed.

"Some of them are. Orchids and other plants live on the tops of these big trees. That way they can get sun. There are many plants up there that we don't yet know anything about," Mom said.

Nate looked up at the gigantic trees. "I know why. Those trees don't have lower limbs. Climbing them would be hard," he said.

Dr. Kidd nodded. "It would be like climbing a 10 to 12 story building. So we only see these plants when a tree falls to the ground. They fall with it," she said.

"Why did it fall?" asked Nell.

"It was old or had a disease," Mom told her.

She kicked at one of the branches. It was alive with insects.

"The termites and other insects are at work eating the tree. That's nature's way of getting rid of dead things. Now the sun will shine on the forest floor and other tree seeds will pop open. They will grow up and fill that hole in the canopy. That's the way the forest continues year after year," Mom said.

The Kidds walked around the tree. Nate and Nell raved about the flowers. Mom took notes. Time went by quickly.

"Soon it will get dark," Torbi called.

"Then we had better go. The rain forest is an exciting place at night. But it can be scary, too. It's easy to get lost in the dark. Also, that's when the animals hunt," Dr. Kidd said.

Nell hurried over to Torbi. "Are there any snakes around here?" she asked.

"Yes, there may be some hiding here now," he answered.

Nell looked around. She shivered.

"Most aren't poisonous. But some are. We always watch where we step," Torbi told her.

"What about animals?" Nate asked.

"Not many large animals live in the rain forest. But smaller ones are all around us. They're hidden in the greenery, too," Torbi said.

Nate and Nell searched for animals as they walked home. They saw a few birds in the trees and one monkey, but that was all. The thousands of others were hidden very well.

Torbi's sons were waiting at the village. They were excited.

"We took the tape player you found down to the store. Luis said he ordered four of them for Harve Klumt. They came in two weeks ago," one of Torbi's sons said.

"We think the other three are still hidden out in the forest. One would play for awhile. Then another one would and then the next and the next. That's why we spent all morning searching the forest," the second brother said.

Dr. Kidd nodded. "We've found our robbers. It's Harve and Carl Klumt. They must have been too busy to pick up the record players they left in the rain forest," she said.

"Carl is kind. He's no thief," Nell said.

"Carl has been good to us, too," Torbi said.

Dr. Kidd looked at the dugouts. "Could just one man steal those nuts?" she asked.

Torbi nodded. "Harve could put them in two dugout canoes. He could paddle one and tie the other behind," he said.

"Harve must have the nuts hidden in his house. He'll try to get rid of them. The only boat is Captain José's," Mom said.

Torbi's son spoke again. "Luis says Harve is shipping some boxes to Manaus tomorrow," he said.

Dr. Kidd grinned. "That will be the nuts. We'll be at that boat," she told them.

# CHAPTER 7

## Finding the Brazil Nuts

Two dugouts went downstream the next morning. Nate, Nell, and their mother were in one. Torbi and his two sons were in the other. They were headed for Port Sagra.

Nell raved about the dugout ride. "I liked visiting Jan and her parents. But this is more fun than riding in the jeep. The road was slick and muddy. We nearly got stuck," she said.

"That's what happens to a road in the rainy season," her mother told her.

*Two dugouts went downstream the next morning.*

At last they came to the bigger stream. The two dugouts were still pulled up on the bank.

"Who owns those boats?" Mom asked Torbi.

"They belong to the Klumts. See, the road comes almost down to the water," Torbi said.

They paddled over to the shore. Nate got out and walked to a dugout. Something was on the bottom of the boat. It was a Brazil nut. "Look what I found," he said.

Dr. Kidd showed it to Torbi and his sons. "It's just as we thought. Harve brought the nuts here," she said.

"This was a good place to leave his jeep," Torbi said.

Mom nodded. "Harve loaded them into the

jeep from the dugouts. Then he took them to his house. Today he's sending them to Manaus. But he'll pretend something else is in the boxes."

They paddled on to Port Sagra. Captain José's boat was coming upstream. Two jeeps were parked by the dock. Carl and Harve unloaded boxes.

Dr. Kidd climbed up on the dock. "That's a lot of boxes. What's in them?" she asked.

Harve didn't seem happy to see Mom but he forced a smile. "I'm sending lots of dishes and lamps and things to Manaus. My friend needs them for her apartment," he said.

"Are you sure that's what's in them?" Dr. Kidd asked.

Harve's face turned red. "Of course, I am," he said. He started forward with a box.

Mom held up her hand. "Show us."

Carl looked puzzled. "Doctor Kidd, what's going on?" he asked.

"Yes, what is going on?" called Captain José. He had docked his boat and stood watching.

"Someone stole Torbi's harvest. We think Harve has the nuts in those boxes," Mom said.

"That's not so. I told you what's inside," Harve said.

"Then show us. Or the boxes can't come on my boat," Captain José said.

"O.K.," said Harve. He reached inside a

box and pulled out a lamp. "See, what did I tell you?" he said.

"That's a big box. What else is in there?" Dr. Kidd asked.

"Just packing to keep things from breaking," Harve answered.

Mom stepped closer and pushed her arm deep in the box. She pulled out a handful of nuts. "Here you are, Torbi," she said.

Carl gasped. "I'm sorry, Torbi. Harve, how could you do such a thing?" he demanded.

Harve's mouth trembled. "I had to make Torbi sell. It's the only way the cattle company will buy our farms. Otherwise, we're going to lose them," he said.

"There are worse things than losing a farm. I can't believe you did that to Torbi," Carl said.

"Why not let Torbi buy your land? He could pay a little after each harvest," Mom said.

"That is better than we deserve after what Harve did," Carl said.

Now Torbi spoke up. "The land and my family will be happy, too. We will help the trees come up. Plants and animals will live there, and one day it will be a rain forest again."

Dr. Kidd smiled at his friend. "Torbi, you're a good ecologist," she told him.

Nate and Nell smiled. "And we know what that means. Ecology is man and nature working together," they said.

This book must be returned on or before the last date stamped below.